Dear Sam,

Happy Reading.
Soon you'll be reading
to your new brother & a
lots of love &

Aunt Penny & Uncle Neil

July 1985

Higgledy Piggledy

THE HEN WHO LOVED TO DANCE

For Joshua, who also loves to dance,
and for my parents, Sondra and Mayo
FS

To my nephew André
EM

First published in Great Britain by
HarperCollins Publishers Ltd in 1995
10 9 8 7 6 5 4 3 2 1
Text copyright © Francesca Simon 1995
Illustrations copyright © Elisabeth Moseng 1995
A CIP catalogue record for this title is available
from the British Library.
The author and illustrator assert the moral right
to be identified as the author and illustrator of the work.

ISBN: 0 00 198065-3

Printed and bound in Hong Kong
This book is set in 19/28 New Baskerville

Higgledy Piggledy

THE HEN WHO LOVED TO DANCE

Francesca Simon
Illustrated by Elisabeth Moseng

Collins
An Imprint of HarperCollinsPublishers

Higgledy-Piggledy didn't
lay eggs like her mother
or crow cock-a-doodle-doo
like her father.
Higgledy-Piggledy danced.

Hour after hour, day after day, Higgledy-Piggledy practised her pirouettes,

twirling and whirling across the farmyard.

The other animals thought Higgledy-Piggledy
was a silly, lazy, good-for-nothing hen.
"Why don't you do something useful?"
said Calypso. "I catch mice."

"I pull the cart," said Festival.

"I give milk," said Lily.

"I make wool," said Delilah.

"I lay eggs," said Big Blanche.

"I provide down and feathers," said Dilly.

"I protect you all," said Towser.

Everyone looked at Higgledy-Piggledy.

"I dance," said Higgledy-Piggledy.

Even Higgledy-Piggledy's mother said there was no future in it. "Whoever heard of a dancing hen?"

But Higgledy-Piggledy just went on practising her twirls and high-steps, trying to spin on one leg without falling over.

"Time you stopped dancing and started laying," said Calypso. "My Max is no older than you, and look what a good mouse-catcher he is."

"1-2-3, 1-2-3, 1-2-3," muttered Higgledy-Piggledy, waltzing into the duck pond.

One hot summer day Dilly started honking.

"Help! Help! Help!"

All the animals ran into the farmyard.

"What is it? What's wrong?" asked Festival.

"Max is in trouble!" shouted Dilly.

Max huddled at the top of the tall oak tree.

"Help!" meowed Max.

"Come down at once, Max," said Calypso.

But Max was too scared to move. "I can't," said Max.
"It's too high. I'm stuck." And he started to cry.

"Don't worry, Max, I'll help you," said Festival,
and he pulled his cart.

"I'll help," said Lily,
and she brought milk.

"I'll help," said Delilah,
and she gave wool.

"I'll help," said Big Blanche,
and she laid an egg.

"I'll help," said Dilly, and she plucked a feather.

"I'll help," said Towser, and he barked.

"I'm slipping," said Max.

"Somebody do something!" screamed Calypso.

Just then Higgledy-Piggledy
pirouetted across the yard.

"Look at me! Look at me! Look at
me!" shrieked Higgledy-Piggledy. "I can do it!"

Round and round twirled Higgledy-Piggledy,
balancing gracefully on one leg. She looked wonderful.

Max forgot he was scared. Max forgot he was high up in the oak tree. Max wanted to dance, too. His paws began to move, and before he knew it he'd danced down the tree.

Then Higgledy-Piggledy and Max
glided round the farmyard together.
"That looks like fun," said Festival.
"I wish I could dance," said Lily.

"All together class. 1, 2, 3, twirl!"
said Higgledy-Piggledy.

"That's my girl," said Big Blanche proudly.